The Wild White Stallion

As Folco paddles his boat along the marshes and waterways of the Camargue, he dreams of horses. His grandfather wants him to become a fisherman, but he sees himself as a cowboy, capturing and taming the wild white horses of the region. His dreams suddenly and unexpectedly come true, however, when he gains the trust of a foal whose mother has been captured by gypsies. *The Wild White Stallion* is an unusual and beautiful account of friendship between a boy and a wild animal, for readers of nine upwards.

René Guillot was born in France and became one of the country's best-known writers for children. In 1964 he received the Hans Christian Andersen Medal for his complete works. He died in 1969. *The Wild White Stallion* is written after Albert Lamorisse's film *Crin-Blanc.*

the *Wild White* *Stallion*

René Guillot
Translated by Gwen Marsh

Illustrated by David Barnett

Beaver Books

First published in Great Britain in 1961 by
George G. Harrap & Co. Ltd.
182 High Holborn, London WC1
First published in France under the title *Crin-Blanc* in 1959 by
Librairie Hachette, distribué par Presse-Avenir

This paperback edition published in 1978 by
The Hamlyn Publishing Group Limited
London · New York · Sydney · Toronto
Astronaut House, Feltham, Middlesex, England

© Copyright Text Librairie Hachette 1958
© Copyright English translation
George G. Harrap & Co. Ltd 1961
ISBN 0 600 39406 9

Printed in England by
Hazell Watson & Viney Limited
Aylesbury, Bucks
Set in Monotype Imprint

Contents

1 The Gypsies

The water has gone down again, thought Folco. Standing barefoot on the rotten boards of his old boat, he felt it scrape on the mud bottom. He knew this awkward spot between the mud-banks.

Indeed, Folco knew all the waterways that ran in and out of the marshes in the Camargue. This land was to him a glorious kingdom, all his very own. Often, in the evening, he would go off on a small voyage of discovery, as he was doing now – alone in his Grandfather Eusebio's boat, like a prince visiting his domains.

This vast country of blue skies and tranquil waters belonged to him, Folco. He was tall and strong, and for a boy of twelve his muscles were unusually hard. He stood up in the stern of the boat, his bare feet lodged against the sides, and plunged his pole firmly into the mud. He passed his fingers through the tangle of hair that was always falling into his eyes; his forehead was running with sweat. Then, bending over the pole, he threw all his weight upon it to move the boat forward.

At last the boat edged out and away from the reeds and slid noiselessly over the silvery water.

This evening he was going to go right across the marsh to the vast plains on the other side; they always attracted him, for there, in broad pasture-lands, lived herds of wild horses. Sometimes Folco would see them galloping over the marsh, their manes flying in the wind, in a haze of sand and sun.

The boy's daydreams were of nothing else; his head was full of these wonderful horses.

Grandfather Eusebio would have liked the boy to be a fisherman, as he was himself. But no, Folco did not want to be a fisherman. When the time came he was going to be a cowboy of the Camargue. There is no finer job than being a cowboy – you are on horseback all day long, galloping in search of the herds of black bulls or capturing and taming wild horses.

The light was fading now. In the darkened sky a flight of flamingoes slowly unfurled like a pink streamer and disappeared in the clouds that veiled the setting sun.

A fresh wind rose, bending the reeds. In less than an hour it would be quite dark.

Folco suddenly noticed how far his boat had

drifted. Never before had he come so far from home. It was time he went back.

Lost in his dreams, the boy had entirely forgotten his special reason for leaving the house that evening ; it was not just to wander about the marsh.

Grandfather Eusebio had told him to take up the nets they had spread together some days before.

I've still got time if I pole hard, thought Folco.

With a heave on the pole he turned the boat about. It was a heavy boat. The water seeped in through the worm-eaten planks. The boy was standing in it up to his ankles. He would have to stop and bail out with the old bucket into which they normally threw the fish they had caught.

Folco pushed over to the bank, and stuck his pole in at the stern to keep the boat in the middle of the reeds.

It was quite by chance that on this particular evening he had gone so far into the marshes and then been forced to stop at just this spot in front of some thick bushes that completely hid the wide plain. Chance alone was leading Folco towards his dearest dream.

He took the battered bucket and knelt down in the boat; but just at that moment he heard a slight noise in the reeds. Some animal had come down to the water to drink. Or perhaps it was the brown otter, whose mocking eyes and busy whiskers had so often delighted Folco before.

He listened. Not a leaf stirred.

In the deep silence of the evening nothing could be heard but the gentle lapping of the water against the sides of the boat.

Then suddenly Folco saw just near him a wavy picture on the surface of the shining water.

The picture grew clearer; a white shape was mirrored there, with two slender ears and two large, dark eyes that kept opening and closing in the ripples.

Folco held his breath; his heart was beating wildly as he got softly to his feet. Very cautiously he drew the high reeds apart.

The picture immediately disappeared from the surface of the water, then as suddenly returned.

Folco could hardly believe his own eyes as he found himself gazing at the reflection of a magnificent foal, stretching its delicate neck through the reeds.

The animal was probably seeing its own reflection in the water for the first time. It was certainly the first time this baby creature from the herd of wild horses had seen a human child. The foal raised its head with a sudden start, flinging back the white crest of its mane. A long shiver ran along its coat of spotless white from mane to tail.

Startled, the young horse stood trembling on its reed-like legs. But it did not run away. It stayed quite still, planted on its four feet in the mud, facing the boy.

And their eyes met.

It was as if the dazzled smile that was on Folco's face fascinated the timorous foal. It opened its big eyes wide, with a look that was gentle and a little sad.

That is how horses look at you when they know you well, when they are your friends. That is how they try to speak to you, dilating their nostrils and making their black lips gently tremble.

Folco was very excited and had only one fear – that he might frighten the little horse away. He dared not move at first. Then, after a time, he felt bolder and, leaning softly forward, he stretched out his hand to try a timid caress.

At once a light glinted in the foal's over-large eyes. The little creature reared up and moved aside. Then, with a leap, off it went head down through the reeds.

It was just as Folco had imagined it in his dreams.

Now the beautiful vision was gone.

The boy pulled himself on to the bank and found there in the drier soil the marks of small hoofs.

He slipped through the bushes and came out on the short, brown grass of the plain.

Barely twenty paces away he saw a tall mare with full, rounded flanks, also entirely white. The strands of her long silvery mane fell over her shoulders. She walked up and down a few steps in this direction, a few in another, stopping here and there to tear at a tuft of grass, while the snow-white foal gambolled about her.

Folco went nearer. He did not think of the time any more, nor of the growing darkness, though he was a long way from Grandfather Eusebio's cottage. His naked feet made no sound on the sand, but the mare scented him approaching. She neighed to call the foal back to her. Immediately it galloped up to her and pressed close to her side.

She's going to run away, thought Folco.

Wild horses are very nervous and shy. They never let anyone come close to them. To his great surprise Folco saw that the mare did not seem at all frightened. She even came a few steps towards him. Then she stopped and watched him.

'My beauty,' said Folco. 'You're not afraid of me, are you?'

He was very close now. The mare stretched her long white face out to him, sniffing as if she would have liked to nibble the boy's untidy mop of hair.

'There, there, my beauty ... let me stroke you. . . .'

Folco ran his fingers through the silky mane. The mare bent her head down as low as his shoulder.

But it was the handsome foal that Folco really wanted to stroke. It was as wild and restless as its mother was gentle. It kept making rushes at him, trying to bite him but still staying close to its mother. And the mare, to reassure her colt, licked its nostrils with her long tongue.

One thing did seem to attract the young colt, however: it was Folco's voice, gentler than any caress.

'There now, White Crest! There ... gently now!'

White Crest! The name came to the boy's lips of its own accord. It suited the foal perfectly, and the animal would soon learn to recognise it.

'Don't be frightened. I'll come back, White Crest. Very soon. I'll come and see you again, and we'll be friends, you and I.'

Folco had barely time left to reach home before night would be upon him. He ran back to the water's edge as fast as he could. There he

jumped into his boat, plunged in his pole, and pushed as hard as he could, so as to get back quickly to his grandfather's cottage.

Folco had no idea that from some distance away, two men had been watching him all the time. Well hidden in the bushes, they waited until Folco was out of sight.

They were gypsy horse-thieves.

Folco's boat had passed only a few yards away from them.

'Are you sure he didn't see us?' said the younger, who was wearing gold earrings.

'You're frightened of everything, even a little kid!' sneered his companion, an old man with grey hair and a sun-tanned face.

'But suppose he's a boy from the ranch . . .?'

'He isn't,' replied the old man. 'The ranch house is over two miles away. We're deep in the marsh here. I know just where we are. I came here two years ago. You've seen how it is, Pedro. We've had a bit of luck; the mare's not nervous – she let the kid get right up to her.'

'Maybe she knows him already.'

'No, no,' said the old man.

'Well, she must be broken in, then: they've ridden her before.'

'Of course, Pedro.'

'The difficult thing's going to be getting rid of the foal,' said the gypsy with the gold earrings.

'You leave the foal to me, Pedro, I'll look after him,' sneered the old man. 'I'm used to them. You get the slip-knot ready on your lasso and give the small rope to me. You know what to do?'

'Yes. But, look! She seems anxious all of a sudden. She's sniffing the air. Has she got wind of us, do you think?'

'No chance of it, Pedro. We're down-wind. It's blowing on to the marsh. No, it's because soon it will be night and the mare will be wanting to join the herd. There's no time to lose.'

'I'm going to creep through the bushes,' said the younger gypsy.

'All right. You go over there and hide ready to cut off her retreat. I'll crawl across to that bunch of trees. See where I mean? Now – is everything clear? You wait for me on this side. I startle the mare. She takes fright. I get hold of the foal before the mother notices that he can't get back to her. You catch one of her legs with your lasso, she comes down, and she's ours. Off you go, Pedro. The boy's a long way off now. . . .'

2 The Capture

But Folco was not a long way off. He had got stuck again on a bad patch between the mud-banks.

The boy decided that it was quicker to jump out and pull, so he leapt on to the side, bare-foot in the mud, tied the rope around his waist, and moved along the bank dragging the boat slowly after him. It was hard work and soon he was sweating, but at last he reached a deeper spot where the boat came free and floated on the water.

Folco took up the pole again. It was then that he heard sounds from the plain beyond the bushes – sounds of a struggle and the muttered oaths of the horse-thieves. A moment later came a long, wild neighing!

In one bound Folco was out of the boat again. He parted the bushes with a wide sweep of his arms. Brambles lashed his face.

On the empty, boundless plain a blanket of mist was spreading, gilded by the rays of the setting sun.

Folco, still some distance away and with the red sun in his eyes, witnessed the big white mare's desperate fight.

Her experience of men was that they had never done her any harm. She had allowed these horse-thieves to come up close to her. Then suddenly she had seen the man who was crawling towards her hurl himself at her foal, knock it down, and roll with it on the ground.

That was when Folco had heard the long, distressing neigh, as the mother dashed to the help of her foal. The lasso whistled through the air and the mare came down in full gallop, one leg caught in the noose.

But where was White Crest? Had he run away? Had he managed to break free?

Folco could not clearly see the men near the clump of trees, for the mare's hoofs were sending up a cloud of dust. She lay on the ground, her feet threshing, and the men rushed up to her.

Folco stood rooted to the spot, overwhelmed by what he saw. He would have liked to rush away, shouting for help. But he was quite at a loss to know what to do. He just stood in the middle of the eerie marshes, barefoot and shivering in his soaking clothes. He could only stare, with rage in his heart, and do nothing ... nothing!

Then suddenly a gleam of hope shot through him.

'She's going to get away!' he muttered.

Twice the proud mare, her leg still held in the painful noose, rolled over on the ground with flailing hoofs, and twice in her wild fury she struggled up again with a powerful thrust of her legs.

The gypsy who had hold of the rope was trying to wind it round a tree-trunk, the better to control the animal, but so far he had not succeeded.

The mare charged him. Rearing on her hind legs, her mane flying in the wind, she came down, pounding the earth, and hurled herself with threatening jaws at her enemies, snapping at them with her teeth.

Folco could hear her rough breathing and the neigh that came from her throat. Head low, she sent one of the men rolling in the dust with a terrible club-like blow. She nearly fell on top of him – he scrambled away just in time. But the mare seized the end of his coat in her teeth and ripped it off.

Another rush . . . and a shout!

Then the other gypsy, the young one who was clinging to the lasso with both hands, fell over backwards.

'Brute!'

Folco saw the man get up painfully, bringing his hands to his stomach. He had dropped the rope – and the mare was free!

Feeling herself no longer tied, the mare instinctively broke into a furious gallop. She could hear the stallions of the herd, far away in the darkness on the other side of the plain, answering her neighing, and in panic and fear she raced off towards the sound.

Folco's heart was pounding so hard he felt it would burst. He thought the mare would escape now for sure; but before the two men could dash in pursuit he saw her come furiously back at them and attack one of them as he threw himself at her head. Pulling up short on all four hoofs, she stopped, neck outstretched, sniffing the wind.

She was searching for her foal.

And he, White Crest – why wasn't he calling for his mother? Was he hurt?

At last the mare heard a moan. She rushed towards it. Too late! The men threw themselves on the rope together. She could not drag both of them along.

This time she was mastered.

Running to the clump of trees, one of the gypsies managed to sling the end of the lasso rapidly round a branch and make the knot safe. Now the mare could struggle for ever, she would not get away. The proud animal had fought to the end of her strength. She was exhausted.

It was quite dark by now. The last ribbon of red was fading on the horizon.

Folco could only see vague shapes in the gathering mist. He did not see the gypsies hauling in the rope little by little until the defeated mare, her mouth covered with foam, was brought in under the trees. There, dodging her attacks and her snapping teeth, her captors at last succeeded in slipping another rope round her nose – a makeshift bridle by which to lead her. Then they released the tied leg, which the rope had chafed raw, and they were able to take her away.

Folco's eyes followed the group as they moved off: the two thin, dark shapes beside the tall, white mare were gradually swallowed up in the grey mist.

Then Folco rushed madly towards the clump of trees, which was nothing now but a dark patch in the middle of the plain.

White Crest had not followed his mother, or Folco would have seen him. He had not been able to escape, so the boy meant to find him – he

23

was somewhere there in the bushes. What had the gypsies done with the little foal to keep him out of the way?

A pool lay in his path but Folco was running too fast to stop. He tore through it, ankle-deep, splashing mud in all directions but hardly slackening his pace at all.

It was night now. In this mist, growing steadily thicker, blotting everything out, the little black trees seemed to be running away into the darkness. At last, with his legs almost giving way under him, Folco came to the first clumps of bushes. He had to stop for a moment to get his breath back.

He listened. There was not a sound . . . only the thumping of his heart against his ribs. Then he called:

'White Crest!'

Some night-bird flew out of the bushes. Then silence again.

'White Crest!'

This time Folco thought he heard a moan. He ran on, caught his foot in the brambles, rolled on the ground and scrambled up again.

Yes, it was a moan he had heard. The foal was there. Folco saw it lying in the bushes with its feet tied together with a rope.

He saw the dark mouth twisted in pain and

fury. The poor creature was at the end of all endurance.

'It's Folco . . . your friend. . . .'

The boy came closer.

The foal turned its head towards him. Its white coat was filthy and in the struggle its nostrils had been badly cut on the thorns. The poor animal was exhausted but had enough strength still to snap ; in those large eyes, fear and anger were equally mixed.

'White Crest, don't be frightened of me.'

The foal, sensitive to his voice, grew a little calmer and after a while seemed quite reassured.

But it was not the same innocent, trusting little horse that had been so ready to let him stroke it before – when it had seen the boy's smiling face mirrored in the waters of the marsh.

This was the foal's first experience of men, and they had been brutal, had bound him up helpless, and left him half stunned. He had suddenly discovered his wild instincts, the natural fear that made him attack.

Folco stretched out his hand to untie him, but drew it back hurriedly. White Crest made a snap at it with his teeth.

'I'm not going to hurt you . . . you know I'm not!'

But the foal was afraid. Its splendid white

chest was heaving; Folco dared not come close. He went on talking in soothing tones:

'There, White Crest ... gently ... it's all right,' and, kneeling on the ground a step or two away, he looked lovingly at the little horse. When the foal's deep fury had abated he would allow himself to be untied. But for the moment the two black eyes afire with rage seemed to say: 'You dare touch me!'

Instinct was very keen in this young creature of the Camargue. Those ropes that the gypsies had used to tie him were his first bonds.

White Crest accepted the boy's presence; he was used to his smell and his voice already. But he did not need Folco's help to free himself. He began doggedly chewing through the rope, tearing bits away from it and then licking his hurt legs. A glance at Folco ... then the foal went on sawing through the hempen rope with his teeth.

'I see you've got your teeth already,' said Folco with a laugh. 'And you certainly know how to use them, don't you?'

At last the rope broke.

With one leap White Crest was on his feet again. Folco stood up too. The foal's head came up to his shoulder.

The boy realised that this was the moment of

their first real meeting – the moment of friendship.

The foal was alone now, lost in the depths of the marsh without his mother. Fear of being abandoned made him tremble; his eyes reflected his distress.

The night was dark, the sky was without stars.

'White Crest!'

Would the little horse follow him or not?

'Come with me . . . come on . . .'

The foal sniffed at the air just as the mare had done before.

Folco walked a few steps as if he were going away.

'Come along, White Crest . . . come with me . . .'

Oh, wonderful! Timidly, hesitating at every step, the little horse followed Folco. He was no longer afraid.

The boy walked backward, softly calling to his friend all the time. They soon came to the thicket where the fight had taken place.

Suddenly White Crest stopped. He stretched his neck, twisted his head this way and that, standing stiff and still on his long legs with his back turned on the marsh. Then, all at once, as the boy watched, the foal dashed away in full flight.

There was no way to stop him; he was already too far away to hear the boy's desperate call. Nose to the wind, galloping as fast as he could, the little wild horse sped on in the track of his mother stolen by the horse-thieves. Soon he was no more than a tiny white patch disappearing into the night.

Folco was left alone in the middle of the plain, with the wind sighing in the reeds of the Camargue marshes. Sad at heart, the boy returned to his boat.

At home they would be worried by his long absence. Grandfather Eusebio and Folco's little brother would be relieved to see him back.

He must go quickly . . . quickly!

Folco ran as fast as he could, jumped into the boat, and pushed away furiously with the pole. From a long way away, as he reached the bend in the long channel of water, he saw the light from the cottage shining in the darkness.

He wondered, should he tell them at home of the incredible adventure he had had that evening out in the marsh . . .?

3 Antonio

Folco decided he would tell only Rico, his little brother – after supper, when the candle had been blown out and they were lying side by side under the blankets.

And, of course, he would tell the story to Antonio.

Antonio, an old cowboy, was Folco's friend. He had finished his term of service with the rancher, but they still kept a place for him there. He used to sleep on the straw in the stables near the horses he loved; there he was happy. Folco had only once been to visit Antonio. Then he had seen the grand house where the rancher lived, the owner of the herds of wild horses. Usually Antonio and the boy met when the old cowboy went riding out to visit the herds, because then he often made a detour to have a chat with his old friend Eusebio.

Several days had passed since Folco had met White Crest on the night the gypsies stole the big white mare.

One day, at sunrise, there came the familiar bang of a hatchet on the door. Folco was crouching by the hearth, blowing on the embers to liven up the fire and brew the early morning coffee. He ran eagerly to open the door.

'Hello, Antonio . . .'

'What! The house not awake yet! Hold my horse, lad, and help me climb out of this saddle. You know me – I get stuck in it like a stone in the bottom of a bag!'

Antonio was nearly crippled with rheumatism nowadays, and was unable to mount or dismount without help.

'I've come to have breakfast with you,' he said.

Franqui, the horse, was tied to the metal ring that served as a door-knocker, and Antonio dragged his stiff legs into the house, calling: 'Come on! Up you get, Eusebio! Out of it, now! Oh, so you're up, are you? 'Morning to you! Give me a stool, will you, lad? Well, anything new on the marsh this time?'

'Only the same old things, Antonio. What about you? Anything over your way at that devil of a rancher's?'

'Don't talk to me about devils, Eusebio! The devil *has* been our way – dressed in rags. Yes – gypsies!' he nodded. 'Somebody's stolen a mare that had a fine little foal.'

'White Crest!' cried out Folco.

'What did you say, lad?'

'I saw the gypsies myself, Antonio. I saw them the night they stole the mare. I was there in the marsh, just by them.'

'If you listen to him he'll tell you a lot of wild stories, Antonio,' laughed Grandfather Eusebio. 'The young rascal . . . and it's all your fault, too!'

'My fault?'

'Yes, that's what I said. You're the one who has turned his head with your everlasting talk about horses! And you know it!'

'Let the boy talk, though, Eusebio,' said the old cowboy. 'I've told you often enough what I think. You're making a mistake to go against the boy. Folco's got horses in his blood. He's going to make a splendid cowboy one day.'

'Never!' cut in Eusebio.

'Who can say "never" like that, Eusebio? Anyway, let's not argue about that now. . . . One thing's certain: the mare's lost; we won't see her again. It was Marco used to ride her. You remember Marco, Eusebio? He's making the most of his retirement now. A nice house and vineyard over by Arles. The mare, Rita, was slightly lame, so the rancher had her put back in the herd. A splendid mare she was. . . . Ah, well! There's nothing to be done but accept the fact that she's gone. But the worry is the foal! If only he, at least, could be found. . . .'

'So that's why you're out searching at the crack of dawn?' said Grandfather Eusebio.

'Yes. I'm looking for the foal. Oh, I know . . . there's not a chance of finding him, of course! Still . . . Would you mind lending me your boy for the day, Eusebio? I like some company when I'm out on the marsh.'

'Oh, yes! Will you, Grandfather?' begged Folco.

'Go on, then, you young scamp. I'll walk a bit of the way with you. I'm just going along to my plot.'

That was the way the old fisherman always referred to his small field, some five hundred yards from his house.

They left at last, Folco helping Antonio into the saddle. Then the boy leaped up lightly behind.

Eusebio walked along beside them, his spade over his shoulder. And perched on the blade, beak in the air, was Grandfather's tame lark, his constant companion.

In his youth Grandfather Eusebio had wandered about the world and across the far seas; it was in China that he had learned how to catch and tame wild birds.

When he came to his field Eusebio took the bird in his hand and threw it into the air. It flew off and disappeared.

The old man would stay several hours digging on his plot of land. Then, before going back to his cottage, he would whistle loud and long with two fingers in his mouth. And immediately, the tiny lark that was lost on high would drop like a stone out of the sky and perch on the old man's shoulder.

'Have a good day, Antonio.'

'We'll have something to eat out in the pasture,' said the old cowboy. 'I'll bring the boy back home to you this evening.'

Folco and his old friend went away along the edge of the marsh in the direction of the wide, bare, desolate plain.

'Do you think White Crest is really lost, then?' asked Folco anxiously.

'He'll have run as far as his legs will carry him, you can be sure of that.'

'Then what, Antonio?'

'Then he'll have fallen down exhausted. Young horses are very delicate, you know.'

'He was such a beauty,' murmured Folco with a sigh.

'I know, my boy. I saw him once. Not a spot on his coat – pure white. Even his mane was as pure as snow. With a bit of luck, of course . . .'

'Oh, do you think there's a chance, Antonio?'

'Yes, of course, my boy. You have to trust your luck, you know. Look – there's the herd, and a very fine herd it is, too. They're at their games. Look at the way they're running! That's to teach the young ones to stretch their legs.'

The herd of white horses passed them like a streak of lightning. Not a foal trailed behind. The stallions set the pace, and the young ones followed the mares.

'We'll see them again tonight by the river,' said Antonio, 'when they come to drink. The sun's not too high yet. We'll go on as far as the plain.'

At noon the old cowboy and Folco got down from Franqui's back and had their meal – bread and cheese and some dried figs – that Antonio had brought in his bag. Then they drank from a goatskin wine-bottle, holding it high above their mouths and pressing the moist bag to make the wine flow between their lips.

'And now we'll have a little nap, eh, my boy?'

Folco would have liked to go on.

'You must have a rest, lad. The sun's very strong. Stretch out in the grass and don't think of anything.'

That was easily said, but how could Folco

stop thinking about White Crest! Since that first meeting, the little white horse had been constantly in his thoughts. How the boy longed to have the colt for his friend!

And yet, tired by the long hours of riding about the marsh, Folco soon fell asleep.

He was awakened at the same moment as the old cowboy himself by the whinnying of Antonio's horse; he looked across to where it was tethered among the trees.

'Whom are you talking to, Franqui?' said Antonio. 'Or is it the horse-flies biting too hard? Quiet, now!'

'Antonio! . . .'

'Yes?'

'Look, Antonio!'

'What is it, lad?'

'There – look, over there, Antonio!' Folco pointed to a clump of reeds across by the marsh, a green patch on the scorched plain where the sunlight was like a dazzling dust.

'I can't see anything,' said Antonio, shading his eyes with his hand against the sun, 'though my sight isn't what it was. What can you see, Folco?'

'White Crest . . .' whispered the boy, almost too excited to speak. 'Rita's foal. He's going

down to the ditch, and our Franqui scented him
from a distance. He called him. . . .'

A second time the old cowboy's horse gave a
whinny that carried far.

'The foal's coming this way, towards us,
Antonio. He's found his herd's pasture-lands
again. I'm sure it's White Crest!'

They could hear a thin, trembling quaver
answering Franqui's call.

'You stay here, Folco!' ordered Antonio,

holding the boy back by the arm or he would have dashed forward to meet the little horse.

'Stay here by me, and don't move.'

'But he's limping, Antonio!'

'No, he isn't. He's just worn out. You're quite right, my boy – it's our foal.'

'I was sure it was White Crest.'

'What a state he's in, too!' said the old cowboy with a grunt.

Now that he was a little closer they could see better what several days of wild chasing in search of his mother had done to the magnificent young colt.

It certainly was White Crest, but not a hair on his body was still white. His whole coat was muddy and filthy. The foal's tail hung down as

stiff and dry as a piece of rope. His neck strained forward, his head hung low, as if it had grown too heavy for him. He was dragging his hoofs along the ground and could not possibly have run another step.

At Franqui's new call, White Crest raised his head. He was still proud as he faced the old horse. He whinnied, stopped, and scratched at the earth with his hoof.

'Ah! If he takes after his mother . . .!' said the old cowboy proudly. 'What a noble animal she was! I doubt if we've ever seen her equal. She was queen of the herd in her day. Look at that foal's bearing! And yet he can hardly stand.'

'Let me go up to him, Antonio,' said Folco.

'No!'

'Let me talk to him, then. Please, Antonio!'

'No, let him talk to his big brother here. He's been a long way, you know; and if he has anything to say, it is not to us men he'll say it. He's been through a terrible ordeal – he won't forget it for a long time!'

Folco later on was to remember these words spoken by the old cowboy, who knew his Camargue horses so well.

'You see, Folco, Franqui's just talked to him. And by tonight White Crest will have joined his wild brothers of the herd again. Tonight he'll go and drink with them at the river. And have a bath, too, I dare say – he needs one!'

'Are you sure he's not injured, though, Antonio?'

'You're not going to teach me how to judge a horse's walk, are you, lad? Just look at him now! The scent of his own herd has put new life into him. A hop, skip, and a jump, and he'll be as good as new! There's nothing wrong with that fellow!'

'Isn't he a beauty, Antonio?'

'He certainly is,' said the old cowboy. 'He's going to make a leader. Now, into the saddle again. We're going back. You're feeling happier now, aren't you?'

'Oh, yes, much happier, Antonio. And was that all true, what you were saying about him?'

'True? Of course it's true! You can take it from me – I know what I'm talking about! That White Crest of yours already carries himself like a lord – he'll be a leader of horses.'

4 The White Prince

A lord and leader, Antonio had said. The old cowboy had lived all his life with the horses of the Camargue. He could watch them running free, and racing or fighting each other, and pick out those of noble stock, the ones who showed pride of race and power to lead.

White Crest, fully grown, was fulfilling all his early promise. He was slimmer than the other colts, his chest was deep and strong, his nervous legs were a parcel of muscles.

'A horse made of iron,' said Antonio proudly.

Above all, he was a horse to fear – hot-blooded and terribly violent. He could never forget that men had torn him away from his mother so young. He had been frightened by everything then: the slightest movement on the marsh, even his own shadow. Men were his enemies. Like the really wild beasts, such as savage boars and foxes, White Crest could scent a man from a long way away.

As soon as the shape of a cowboy was seen on

the plain, White Crest, who led the troop of young horses, would give a whinny and that was the signal for flight. Antonio himself had never managed to get near the horse.

But White Crest always recognised Folco.

Several times, out in his boat, Folco had managed to cross the whole marsh and come ashore on the vast territory where the herds of horses roamed. He would get there in the evening, when the horses came down to the water to drink.

The boy could always pick out his friend from among the rest and would hail him, calling him 'White Crest'. The young horse would answer with a somewhat rough whinny, which was really meant to be gentle. He would come closer, sniffing the air, nostrils dilated; he was attracted, but at the same time full of fear.

Certainly he must have retained some memory of that first meeting of theirs, down by the water, when both were about the same height, boy and horse. But now the horse had grown and looked down upon this small human being who talked softly to him and somehow kept him from running away.

Yet, in spite of the caressing voice and its friendly tone, White Crest would never come farther than the edge of the marsh that marked

the end of the horses' domain, as if to say: 'You
are in the domain of men. We're not of the same
kind.'

So the seasons passed.

Folco, obeying his Grandfather Eusebio's
wishes, hired himself out for the months of one
fishing season on the Rhône.

Every day until nightfall the fishermen would
be casting nets that tore their hands. Then in the
evening they would tie up on the muddy shore
of one of those tiny islands, all tamarisk clumps
and bushes of saltwort, that seem to float in the

river and gently drift along towards the sea.

The fishermen would light their camp-fire to cook their fish-soup, and then, rolling themselves up in their blankets, they would sleep on the grass under the stars.

In spite of his being exhausted from the long day's fishing, it often took Folco a long time to go to sleep. He would lie thinking about White Crest; though far from home, from the marsh and the herds of wild horses, he could not stop thinking about his friend, the white prince.

One evening as they drew up to one of these floating islands with the crew of their little cutter, Folco saw fresh tracks of hoofs in the mud. He mentioned it to the captain of their boat. After supper the men were smoking a last pipe round the fire.

'I don't know a lot about horses,' said the captain, 'but some of 'em, they do say, get a sort of crazy fit that comes over them.'

'You mean they go mad?'

'Yes – on and off. Have whims. Fight like devils. They're so savage and terrifying that the others chase them off and treat them as outlaws. Then there are the solitary ones who keep aloof. They are so proud they want the whole earth to themselves to gallop around in! One fine day they just leave the rest and run off on their own.'

'Have you ever seen them, Captain?'

'Yes, I have. I remember one very big, old horse who used to come to the islands like that. Threw himself into the water, he did, and swam across to one of the little islands. That island must have been like a kingdom to him, a place all his own. And then, after a while, he would go back to the herd.'

Folco thought of his beloved White Crest: what a proud creature he was! How highly strung – quite untamable! White Crest would never tolerate men at all, and might well attempt to impose his own harsh rule on the other horses.

So, as the little fisherman went to sleep on the shore, he liked to picture in his mind the white horse swimming across the water, out to some desert island in the River Rhône, where no horse had ever set foot before.

5 The Corral

At the end of the fishing season Folco went back home to the cottage. He was glad to see Rico and Grandfather Eusebio again after being away so long. And life returned to its old rhythm once again in the little white cottage beside the marsh.

A few days after Folco's return, Antonio called there. The boy had gone out early in his boat.

'He'll be sorry to have missed you,' said Eusebio.

'To tell you the truth, it's maybe better that way, Eusebio. . . .'

'More horse stuff, I suppose,' growled the old fisherman. 'I thought the boy would grow out of it – but his head's still full of nothing but horses. Especially that White Crest!'

'I know, Eusebio.'

'Going already?'

'Yes,' said Antonio. 'I'm off to join all the others. Old as I am, I'll show the rancher that I can earn my keep, on a day like today anyway. There's going to be some sport, today. . . .'

He had an odd look that did not seem to encourage questions. Old Eusebio sat silently in front of the cottage mending his nets, and watched Antonio trot away in the direction of the pastures.

Folco, out on the marsh, was happy – unaware that the rancher and his men were going to try to capture a young horse that day, and that the horse was White Crest!

Antonio caught up with the cowboys just as they were starting to surround the herd of wild horses. The cowboys were superb horsemen, and they all rode swift stallions that could 'eat up the wind', as the saying goes.

Franqui, Antonio's horse, like his master, was growing old and had lost his youthful spirit. But the old cowboy handled his horse so cleverly and neatly that the two always found themselves in the lead. It was an extraordinary zigzag chase through the herd of excited horses, dispersing them and heading off the one they wanted.

'Antonio!' shouted the rancher. 'You go on ahead! The rest stay by the ditch! Now! He's yours! Ride, can't you? What's got into you?'

White Crest was about to escape again. The cowboys galloped in all directions to keep the main part of the herd away and prevent the stallion from jumping the ditch.

White Crest, separated from the herd, made an abrupt turn. But Antonio was coming back again across his path and, to stop White Crest's headlong dash, he reined in his own horse so violently that it nearly fell.

A buck ... a sudden kick, full in Franqui's chest ... and White Crest bolted away at top speed.

He could see in the distance the herd in flight, and in between him and them, the cowboys were riding back, barring his way.

'Jump, Antonio,' shouted the rancher.

But there was no need to strain one's lungs shouting orders to an old cowboy who knew his job so well!

Antonio took off for the jump at the same time as White Crest. The ditch was wide. Terrified by the shouts of the cowboys charging him, and unable to throw off Franqui, whose rider now held him firmly in line, White Crest jumped the ditch with one enormous leap, his flank almost touching Antonio's boot. He landed in the mud, tore himself out of it again, and went speeding on.

But the magnificent stallion could not escape his pursuers any longer.

Antonio reined in his horse to let him get his breath. Now it was up to the younger cowboys. They were hemming in the stallion on all sides; he could not hope to outdistance them now. From this point on, the rancher's riders guided the wild chase across the plain.

As Antonio had said, White Crest had a chest of iron. The cowboys' horses were worn out keeping up with him. The stallion went at a tremendous speed, his splendid mane trailing in the wind, his tail plumed out like a white flame.

He charged the bushes with his chest and drove straight through them. He jumped over quagmires and dashed across the shallows covered with white flowers, where the thin layer of water did not even cover the tips of his hoofs.

But the cowboys never lost contact. Their horses knew where they were going. The house and stables of the rancher were not far away now, hidden by the trees, just beyond the bend in the long, bare clearing where their hoofs hammered over the hard, dry ground.

One last effort for the last lap of their ride.

'Hey! The gates!' yelled the rancher.

They were open, waiting.

The track led into a corral; around a huge,

bare stretch of land was a fence of posts and poles forming an enclosure, and this was the training-ground.

White Crest was caught.

He tried hurling himself madly at the fence, but it held and he fell back, rolling on the ground, bruised and battered. Up he got again immediately and dashed once more around the track, close to the fence all the way, looking for a way out.

The cowboys dismounted and stood behind the palisade watching him. One of them climbed on top and succeeded in throwing a rope round White Crest's neck. Then he jumped down into the enclosure. Now the other cowboys scrambled over the palisade and ran to help their comrade.

The man was agile enough but it was not long before he found himself in a difficult position. Never in the memory of ranchers had they captured a horse who had so much fight in him.

White Crest kept struggling desperately, half strangled by the noose around his neck. Once again here were men torturing him. Broken-winded and almost at the end of his endurance, the proud stallion gathered his strength for one last effort and leaped.

'Keep away! Keep away!' shouted Antonio,

coming up with the rancher. The cowboy who still had hold of the rope was flung rolling in the dust.

'Do you want to be killed?' yelled Antonio.

White Crest, absolutely panic-striken, might well have pounded the man to pieces with his hoofs or torn him to bits with his teeth.

Luckily the horse succeeded in breaking the rope.

Suddenly the rancher shouted, 'Have you lost your wits? Antonio!'

Antonio, having clung to the palisade to help himself dismount, was on the ground and had opened the gate of the enclosure.

'You fool!'

'Would you rather the horse broke his neck, then?' asked the old cowboy. 'The poor beast is out of his mind. It's the purest luck he hasn't come to grief already!'

White Crest now had noticed the exit open to him and hurled himself headlong out of the enclosure. He rushed past only two feet from the rancher and made for the track through the clearing. In a cloud of dust he disappeared at the turning beyond the trees.

'A good day's work!' said the rancher.

'It might easily have been worse!' muttered Antonio between his teeth.

'What're you mumbling about?'

'Nothing, boss. Nothing. . . .'

'Well, stop muttering like an old man,' said the rancher. And to the cowboys he said: 'Take your horses to the stables. They'll have another heavy day tomorrow. But this time, Antonio, we'll get that great white demon. We've mastered worse ones than him before now. Just wait till I have him with a bit between his teeth and a good pair of spurs. . . . Unless you want to have the first ride yourself, Antonio!'

The cowboys laughed.

The young cowboy whom White Crest had nearly injured slept in the stables, as Antonio did. That evening the two of them were talking.

'It's easy to make fun of an old man,' said Antonio.

'I didn't make fun of you, Antonio. . . .'

'No, because you were afraid of that horse, weren't you? And quite right too. You needn't be ashamed to admit it. In my young days I once had to tackle a horse like this one. I remember it only too well. A proud animal, quite untamable. We never did master him. The boss is the one who decides, of course – but if I were him I wouldn't go looking for trouble.'

'The boss is a headstrong and obstinate man, Antonio.'

'I know,' said Antonio, 'I know.'

6 When Dreams Come True

The next day Folco was up early and put on the coffee. Before waking his grandfather, he quickly swept the earth floor of the room.

Eusebio's little lark was still asleep with its feathers all fluffed up, perched as always on a large chest with copper hinges that stood by the old man's bed.

'Up already, Folco?'

'The sun's quite high, Grandfather.'

'Ah, I'm growing old, I'm afraid. It's in my legs now – I'm as bad as Antonio. You'll have to go fishing without me again today. Just take the small net – the other one's falling to pieces, anyway. It'll have to be repaired mesh by mesh nearly.'

'When Antonio goes to Arles,' said Folco, 'we might be able to get him to bring a new one.'

'A new net's expensive, my boy. Anyway, we'll have to see.'

'Coffee's ready, Grandfather.' He turned

towards the bed where his small brother Rico lay. 'Shall I leave him to sleep on?'

'Yes, leave him.'

'I'll probably go on beyond the big lake today.'

'Yes, that's right. There's a lot more fish farther on. But that means you won't be back before nightfall.'

'I'll take some food in my bag,' said Folco.

'Right. Good fishing, my boy.'

Folco slung the bag over his shoulder and went out of the cottage. The boat had again shipped a lot of water overnight and he had to bail it out. Then he pushed off and began poling the boat along.

There would certainly be some fish caught in the nets which he had not taken up the night before. Two hours in the big lake, and with any luck his fish-bucket would be full. Then he would be free until night came and he could go to the pastures, and perhaps catch a glimpse of White Crest.

Little did he suspect that he would be meeting his friend much nearer home than that.

Folco moved on noiselessly, pushing his boat through the masses of white flowers that covered the surface of the pools. He was delighted to have the whole of this long day in front of him.

He came to the mudbanks and stopped to take up two nets full of flashing fish. A fine eel with a pure white belly almost slipped out of his grasp. But luckily it fell on the floor of the boat, where it slid into a corner and could not get away.

Folco went farther on and spread his nets again. As he went past the blue ditch he cast his net twice, and was very lucky each time.

The day was beginning well.

Folco cut through the wide plain of flowering waters; it was as if someone had scattered handfuls of snow, but the snowflakes were the tiny white heads of the flowers.

A bird rose into the air. As he looked up to follow its flight Folco suddenly saw a tall white shape standing out against the background of the bushes. . . .

White Crest!

It was White Crest, resting now from the wild chase of the previous day and his battle with the men. He must have spent the night in this spot, sheltered by the thickets, standing with the water up to his hocks. His mane was all tangled; the thick strands of hair that hung over his forehead covered his eyes and half obscured his face.

White Crest had sensed someone approaching.

He turned his head towards Folco and must immediately have recognised his friend, for he made no move to escape. Suddenly he threw back his head, tossing his mane. His legs stiffened and he drew himself up to his full height. How superb he looked!

The horse had just heard in the distance the sound of steps in the water . . . and then shouts.

'There he is! That's him! We've got him this time! This way, all of you!'

The rancher came galloping up, rallying his men. The water flew up beneath the hoofs of the horses as the cowboys dashed to surround White Crest.

Folco stopped his boat. He would see everything. It would soon be over.

To the great astonishment of the cowboys, the wild stallion made not the slightest attempt to escape. It was his proud blood that spoke in him. He turned to face the horsemen. They all immediately spaced out and took their lassos from the pommels of their saddles.

'He's mine!' shouted the rancher, who was about to hurl his lasso.

But he never had time to throw it.

Sending up a volley of mud that splashed his coat all over, White Crest gave a savage neigh and flung himself at the rancher. It was a terrible attack.

The two horses reared and faced each other. They were on a narrow strip of firm ground that was almost dry. White Crest snapped at his adversary and fought with his hoofs, driving back the rancher's mount. The man himself had dropped the reins to cling to his mare's mane. She was a brave and powerful beast, that mare. She withstood the shock of collision, swerved clear, and fell back heavily on to her feet.

The cowboys came hurrying to the rescue.

But White Crest, beside himself with rage, charged again. The rancher's mare reared so suddenly that her rider was unseated and thrown out of the stirrups on to the ground.

He cursed violently, and the cowboys rushed to pick him up.

'Leave me alone!'

'No bones broken?'

'Leave me alone, I said!'

His voice shook with rage as he got to his feet.

They had to hold the mare by the bridle and steady her, for she was so frantic, she would let no one mount her. But at last the man was able to put his foot in the stirrup, take the reins, and remount.

'Nasty brute!' he cried.

He was choking with fury. He wiped the dripping sweat from his forehead with his shirt-sleeve. Then, shaking his fist in the direction in which White Crest had fled as soon as he had taken his revenge, the rancher shouted: 'The brute! Anyone who wants him can have him!'

Folco heard these words. He went closer. The men all watching him made him feel timid, yet he found the courage to say softly to the rancher, who was blind with rage:

'Do you mean *I* could have him? Would you give him . . . to *me*?'

The boss of the horsemen looked down from his high seat on the mare at this barefooted, shock-headed boy dressed in thin, made-over clothes: a poor, worn shirt and patched, outgrown trousers.

'Who is this little savage?' he asked.

'It's Folco,' answered one of the cowboys.

'Folco . . . Never heard of him.'

'Eusebio's grandson – the fisherman.'

'Oh! Antonio's friend! I see!' sneered the rancher. 'And so this barefoot little ragamuffin wants my horse, does he? And he's not shy, either! Well, yes . . . All right! You can have that horse, kid. But you'll have to *catch* him first – and I think fish'll have wings before that happens!'

The cowboys roared with laughter at their boss's joke.

'Come on, now, all of you,' said the rancher. 'We'd better get back. . . .'

That nasty smile came into his face again as he looked at Folco still standing there in the mud in front of him; the boy had not budged. Then, jerking his horse's head to turn her, the rancher took the lead and trotted off with his men.

Folco stood there, thoughtful: the rancher had been making fun of him. The rancher was a magnificent horseman, yet White Crest had unseated him. Small wonder then if he laughed at the idea of a fisherboy wanting to capture this horse – the wildest stallion in the whole herd. Oh, yes, he had reason to laugh at the boy.

The rancher had given White Crest to Folco before all his men, and the boy said to himself: 'If I capture him White Crest will be mine.' It was enough to make his twelve-year-old heart overflow with joy. The cowboys were no longer following White Crest. He might not have gone very far.

Folco tied up his boat. He was good at tracking. The stallion's hoofs had made deep marks in the mud. He followed them between the reeds along the bank, then, when they began to fade, along the solid ground.

The horse had stopped here, and pawed the earth. Ah, yes! Then he had turned back towards the shallows, where the white flowers grew.

Suddenly Folco saw him. White Crest was tired. His head drooped and the end of his mane was trailing in the water. Folco stepped closer without a sound. He went forward softly.

'White Crest!'

The horse twitched his ears.

Once again White Crest was willing to pause and listen to that soothing, friendly voice; then he would go back to the herd.

'You're mine, White Crest.' Folco said the words softly to himself, like a promise.

He held in his hand, carefully coiled, the rope which the rancher had left on the ground when he had been thrown from his saddle. In a louder voice, so that the horse would raise his head, he called again:

'White Crest!'

And at once he threw the noose.

The horse was surprised, reared up, and leapt away. He started off at top speed, dragging the boy behind him; Folco fell in the mud, but he still clutched the rope.

Nothing on earth would have made Folco let go. The horse snorted and blew, for the rope was tight around his neck. To try to rid himself of this dead weight that kept bumping along behind him he went faster and faster.

Folco, with his head sometimes under water and blinded with mud, clung with all his might to the rope wound about his wrist. The rough coil was sawing through his skin, but he felt no pain.

The boy was pulled right across the watery plain like this on his stomach, his knees and elbows bleeding, his nose full of mud. It was a feat of endurance that seemed to go on for hours; he felt he would be battered to pieces like a clod of earth in a mill-wheel, but he never let go. At last the horse stopped. The animal was trembling a little. He stretched his neck towards the boy who lay full length on the ground, his hair caked with mud. Out of that blackened face shone two points of light – two bright eyes looked up at White Crest.

A few moments passed. The horse was still nervous and remained unmoving, watching, but the boy returned his gaze with a look of friendship in his eyes.

Folco stood up and slowly approached until he could touch White Crest's shoulder. He stretched out his arm along the stallion's neck and buried his fingers in the silky mane.

For a moment the horse's long white cheek brushed against the boy's muddied face.

For the first time in his life White Crest was really letting himself be stroked.

'Come along, White Crest. . . . Come along.'

Folco had no need to hold the rope. White Crest followed him of his own accord. They walked side by side along the narrow track that led along the side of the marsh homeward.

Homeward! Folco and White Crest were going home together.

'Grandfather! Grandfather!'

'What is it?' asked Eusebio as little Rico, Folco's brother, came running up. The old fisherman was sitting in front of the cottage, plaiting reeds for eel-pots.

'Grandfather, it's Folco – Folco and his horse!'

The child could hardly believe his eyes. He was spellbound. Folco had once told him a wonderful story about his meeting a snow-white colt and seeing the mare stolen by the gypsies. Every night when the two of them were lying side by side under the blankets Folco would go on weaving wonderful tales for his little brother about White Crest, the wild stallion he used to go out to watch for in the middle of the marsh.

63

The Wild White Stallion

For the little boy, who was never allowed far from the house, the marsh was a magic land of genies and fairies.

'One day I'll take you with me in the boat,' Folco promised him. 'Then you'll see.'

'You keep promising . . .' sighed Rico.

Rico would stand alone on the shore, watching his big brother go off to adventure in the mysterious land over the water. Out there, he knew, Folco had secret meetings with a white prince who suddenly appeared before him in the form of a white horse with eyes flashing fire, a horse that talked to him as enchanted creatures do in stories.

That was how Folco's little brother thought of White Crest.

Folco was very good at telling stories. The tales made you go on dreaming and wondering for a long time afterwards; but the story of

White Crest was the most beautiful of them all.

And now, tonight, here was his big brother coming back home actually leading this fairytale horse: a real horse with a spotless white coat. He was even bigger and more splendid than the dream-horse Folco had described in his extraordinary adventures.

'Don't be frightened,' said Folco, laughing as he saw little Rico hanging back. 'Look – it's White Crest. He's mine now.'

This must be the next chapter in the fairy-tale, thought Rico.

'Folco, tell me . . . Folco . . .'

Folco bent down and said softly in his ear: 'Yes, White Crest is mine now. From today on, he belongs to me, see? He's my horse – the rancher gave him to me. I'll tell you what happened. . . .'

'He gave it to you!' said Grandfather Eusebio in a tone of scorn and disbelief. 'Was that what you said? I've only got one good ear, but that's enough if it hears aright. You mean to tell me that the rancher made a present of one of his horses to a little nobody like you!'

'Listen, Grandfather . . .'

'Blah, blah, blah. . . . Don't tell me any more of your rubbish!'

'It's White Crest,' said Folco. 'And the rancher really did give me the horse, Grandfather. Honestly, it's true. Only an hour ago it was, in front of all his men. Antonio'll tell you it's true – he was there!'

'All right. . . . You have horses on the brain. It's always the same. They'll send you out of your mind, if you're not careful. I'll speak to Antonio. What're you going to do with him?'

'Put him in the yard,' said Folco. 'Can I?'

'If you like, I suppose. But one thing's certain – tomorrow you go up to the rancher's and get hold of Antonio. I want to talk seriously to that old madman.'

'Thank you, Grandfather!' cried Folco.

And he dragged his little brother Rico, still spellbound, to the yard, with the docile White Crest following.

'I'll keep him here,' said Folco. 'White Crest, you'll be fine here, won't you? You'll see, you'll be well looked after, and I'll dress your cuts and make them well.'

The horse moved rather nervously.

'He has to get used to us,' explained Folco to his brother. 'See, he's eating out of my hand. You give him a handful of hay, too. Don't be frightened. He's sniffing you because he doesn't know you yet. There, I'm holding him by his

67

white mane. Give him the hay, and stroke his cheek. Careful!'

'He's afraid of me,' said the boy.

'No. He put his head up to sniff the wind. Go and close the gate.'

Folco guessed at once the reason his horse shivered and was restless. Far away in the plain the boy and the horse could just hear the neighing of the herd galloping down to the river to drink.

White Crest let fall the wisp of hay he had started to chew, raised his head and pricked up his ears. His trembling lips drew back and his nostrils dilated as with all his strength the stallion answered the call of his herd.

Folco realised that he would not be able to keep his friend there any longer. The instinct of the horse was stronger than the feeling he undoubtedly had for this boy with the kind hands and gentle voice. He could not resist the urge to join his wild comrades on the plains.

The horse side-stepped to avoid little Rico, who was in his way. Folco sprang towards him but there was no way to stop him. When they had first come into the yard Folco had untied the rope from the horse's neck.

Now White Crest dashed at the gate and knocked it down. He galloped off, cutting right across the plain in the direction of the high pastures to join the proud, wild horses who knew no masters. White Crest was going back among his own kind, back to freedom under the wide Camargue sky, and the exhilaration of wind and speed in endless races across the plain.

Folco was losing his beautiful horse. His heart was heavy and sad. Yet he understood that White Crest could not live with men, not even with the boy who was his friend. He needed the wide open spaces.

He'll never come back, thought Folco.

Little Rico felt his big brother's sadness; he trotted after him dejectedly back to the cottage where Folco set about preparing supper.

'I'll see to it,' said his grandfather, and he poked the fire.

7 The Battle of the Stallions

A few days later, when Antonio called at the cottage, Folco was out fishing. Eusebio was sitting at the table with his lark on his shoulder, and in his hand another bird with its feathers all ruffled.

'He's hurt,' said Eusebio. 'Poor little creature. Look. It's his wing. He came down from the sky this evening with my lark when I was coming back from the fields. They must have met up there somewhere. And I bet mine said to him: 'Come back home with me. There's an old man who's very good at fixing wings – he'll do it for you.' So he came. Now I'm curious to see if he'll be faithful to me like the other one, or if he'll just go off as soon as his wing's better. Ah, well – what's new with you, Antonio?'

'Nothing. I've been up to see the herds – now I'm on my way back. I haven't seen Folco for quite a long time.'

'Tell me, Antonio, what's all this White Crest business? Do you know? What's all this rigmarole about the rancher being generous and giving away a horse to a mere boy? The boy goes and takes it all as literal truth, of course. You ought to talk to Folco, Antonio. He isn't eating or sleeping at all nowadays – not since his horse ran away. *His* horse! Do you mark that?'

'Yes, I'll have to talk to the boy,' said the old cowboy. 'Because the rancher . . .' He paused.

'Well, what were you going to say?'

'Nothing,' muttered Antonio. 'The rancher's the rancher, that's all. We don't see eye to eye at all. I'm one of the old school, you see.'

'You don't mean, Antonio – you're not thinking of leaving the ranch?'

'Yes. Not with any pleasure, mind you. But I love horses, whereas the rancher is nothing but a dealer in horseflesh. And I've told him so to his face.'

'Where will you go to, Antonio?'

'I've written to my friend Marco. He'll find me a job there. I told you, he has a house near Arles. I'll help him with his vineyard. And we'll be able to talk about the good old times together. Ah, well, good-bye, Eusebio.'

''Bye. See you soon, Antonio.'

Leaning on one of the gateposts of the gate which White Crest had broken down when he dashed back to freedom, the old cowboy levered himself awkwardly up into the saddle, then trotted gently off towards the setting sun. He did not meet Folco.

The boy came home very late that night. He had been in his boat across the marsh again. But that evening Folco had searched the pasturelands in vain for a glimpse of White Crest. The plain was empty. Folco could not even see in the darkening distance the powdery haze of golden sand that hangs over the long white line of a galloping herd.

There was no wind; not a tremor stirred the reeds or the frail bushes. A storm threatened.

This was the season of hot blood and savage combats, when the stallions of the herd fought each other without mercy. There was a certain spot which was their fighting-ground. Antonio had often spoken to Folco of the place and told him how the would-be leaders met there and challenged each other.

'They fight for the title,' said Antonio.

For the title of leader. The winner becomes chief, with uncontested authority. His will becomes the law of the herd.

Thunder was beginning to rumble dully over the marsh when Folco, still far from the cottage, pushed on his pole and started back for home. He could hear, muffled by distance, the neighing and noises of combat. If he had been present he would have been proud of White Crest.

'Every inch a lord,' Antonio had once said; he had recognised at the first glance that this young stallion with the brooding look was more fiery-tempered than the rest.

The fighting had been going on for hours. White Crest had soon despatched the horses older than himself, though in their time they had been leaders of the herd. They knew how to fight without wasting strength or breath, and age had taught them cunning. But White Crest threw himself against each one with such spirit that he quickly defeated the veterans.

The only rival worthy of White Crest was a young horse with a jet-black mane. A black blaze gave him a sort of third eye in the middle of his forehead, and the crest of hair that hung down over his eyes was black also.

This was the last fight. Either the black prince or the white prince would be leader of the herd; and they were both equally brave fighters. The herd had gathered upon a small hill where some scraggly bushes grew. Fearfully the mares stood a little apart, pawing the ground with restless hoofs. Alone, face to face, the two stallions stood and defied each other.

White Crest, who had had a bad kick in the

previous fight, was bleeding from a deep cut in his leg. He seemed only the more determined to attack this last adversary and rout him.

At first they made a series of feints, watching each other closely, and every now and then trying to get a hold with their teeth in the other's flesh or letting fly with a sudden kick.

The black prince and the white prince were matched for size. But White Crest's opponent was more heavily made, less rapid, less agile than White Crest. He drew back in order to charge. As in a joust, the two stallions rushed towards each other at a furious gallop. The impact was terrible. With a shrill burst of neighing the two horses struggled up from their knees, faced each other, and began fighting at close quarters.

White Crest's teeth tore the black prince's shoulder, drawing from him a scream of pain. The black horse sank under the force of the attack, and White Crest fell upon him, pounding his back with his hoofs and crushing the enemy beneath his weight.

The black-maned stallion struggled up, broke free, and gathered himself for a fresh assault. He sprang at his adversary, but the white horse stood firm.

It was a whirl of flying manes, hoofs pounding the ground or suddenly flying into the air with the most terrifying kicks.

Now it was the white horse who dominated the fearful battle. He kept leaping at his enemy's neck, and the black prince was visibly tiring. White Crest forced him back, head low, spitting foam and gasping for breath.

It was the end of the fight. The black prince was beaten. Struck down with a shattering blow in White Crest's last attack, and wounded in the chest, he rolled over on the ground, trying to avoid the trampling hoofs. Then he stumbled up and, accepting his defeat, retreated, with one leg dragging painfully, to the group of watching mares, who had not moved throughout the fight.

With his head raised to the sky, White Crest gave a loud whinny: his cry of victory. From that time forward he would be the leader. The herd recognised his supremacy. When, without waiting at all, White Crest put himself at their head and started off slowly towards the river, the others all followed.

It was at that moment that the thunder began to rumble over the marshes. Folco was almost back at the cottage by then; the lamp was already lit.

All night long the rain poured down on the thatched roof of the cottage. The storm wandered in circles above the marsh. Shortly before dawn the rain slackened and ceased. And when the sun appeared again the little bushes swimming in the plain of water in front of the cottage glowed a lovely, new-washed green.

Folco had been up for some time already. He had cleared up a little and revived the fire. Now a grand smell of toast was filling the house.

His younger brother Rico was awake, yawning

and stretching under the bedclothes. The cat came asking for his milk, and grandfather's lark, whose companion, once cured, had flown away, pecked at some crumbs on the old chest.

Folco had had a dream about White Crest, and now that he was awake he was still thinking of the stallion – of how he had gone back to his wild brothers and would soon forget Folco in the beautiful kingdom of the horses.

Suddenly the boy pricked up his ears. He thought he heard steps outside in the grass. The steps came closer. And Folco distinctly heard the voice he loved – he would have known it in a thousand others – that soft, rather plaintive whinny that White Crest gave when Folco stroked him.

The boy's heart leaped. A great joy suddenly swept over him.

White Crest had come back.

Folco ran to open the door.

There stood the magnificent white horse, silhouetted against the morning sun. Slowly the animal raised his head. He was tired out. A troubled gleam came and went in the depths of his great, dark eyes.

'It's you . . .' murmured Folco.

He took his friend's head in his arms and pressed it to him. He was so moved that tears of joy welled up in his eyes.

Little Rico came up to the door and stood next to his elder brother.

'He's come back ... of his own accord!' Folco kept saying, both arms about his horse's neck. 'He's come right across the marsh and found the way to our house.'

'What's happening?' asked his grandfather in a husky voice.

'It's White Crest!' cried little Rico. 'White Crest's come back! He's out here. Come and look at him, Grandfather.'

The whole house was upside-down. The toast burnt. The cat helped himself to the bowl of milk. But Folco and his little brother forgot everything in their excitement. They could not get over their wonder and surprise. It was some time before Folco noticed the horse's wound. He saw White Crest stretch out his neck to lick his leg, and realised then that blood was oozing from a long cut, which was open down to the pastern.

'Quick! We must dress his wound. You've been fighting, White Crest, haven't you? Fighting the other horses, and you've been hurt. That's why you've come back. Come along with me.'

White Crest let himself be led, docilely, into

the small fenced yard behind the house. This time Folco did not even trouble to close the gate.

He must be quick and dress the wound. He ran for a bucket and brought it back filled with water. Then, tearing a strip off his shirt, he began to sponge the cut.

'Give me your leg!'

White Crest did not seem to mind, but did whatever Folco wanted; he bent his knee, and the boy took the hoof in his hand.

'There . . . put your foot in the bucket. That's better. Now, don't move.'

The two boys knelt at the horse's feet and delicately cleaned the cut. It was deep, and full of the gravel and earth churned up during the fight.

'There, isn't that better, now?' said Folco.

He continued bathing the leg for some time, for it was hot and inflamed. Then with a very clean white cloth that his brother had gone to fetch from the chest, he bandaged it round and tied it firmly with string.

White Crest whinnied with satisfaction.

'You see, he's happy,' said Folco to the little boy. 'And this time he won't go away again. I'll go and get him a bundle of hay.'

That day Folco did not go fishing. His old

grandfather, groaning, and cursing his bad leg, decided he would try to go himself to spread the nets. It gladdened the old man to see such joy in the children's eyes. So off he went with his little lark perched on his shoulder.

'Have a good day, boys. Are the nets where I told you to leave them. Folco?'

'Yes, just before you come to the lake.'

'See you tonight, then.'

The boat glided away.

We talk of choosing friends, but I often wonder if it is really choice or chance that guides us. . . . It seems as if choice must come into it. We single out the friend at once, be he man or animal. Folco's friend was this big horse from the marshes of the Camargue. From the very first the boy had loved White Crest, and taken him to his heart.

Folco would never forget that wonderful day and the week that followed. For his little brother it seemed just as if their fairy-tale was going on and on.

Folco was blissfully happy. The rancher had made him a present of the best horse in the herd. But more than that, White Crest had made a present of himself. It was from pure friendship that he was still there with them at the cottage.

He would run up as soon as Folco called him. He ate out of his hand. He would have followed him into the house, even. He sometimes poked his head right through the door, but his shoulders jammed in the narrow opening.

All Folco's dreams now were of mounting his horse and dashing off on long, long rides across the marshes. But so far he had never dared to try riding him.

Once the leg-wound was reknit, Folco removed the bandage and tied a bunch of leaves to the horse's hock to keep away the flies.

Almost a week had gone by in this friendly fashion when one morning Antonio called at the cottage. White Crest, on the other side of the fence, answered Franqui's noisy greeting with a joyful neigh.

'Do you see, Antonio?' shouted Folco, running out to meet his friend.

The old cowboy let the reins drop on his own horse's neck, and the two animals were soon rubbing noses over the top of the fence.

'It's White Crest, Antonio! See him?'

'No, I don't see him . . .' said Antonio rather gruffly. 'I've not seen a thing.'

He might have added that it was no business of his to report back to the rancher what he had seen, amazing though it was: first a Camargue horse normally terrified of men obeying a mere boy as if they had always lived together ... then, a little ragamuffin, as the rancher had called him, brimful of happiness.

Folco, the poor fisherman's son in rags and tatters, was as handsome as a prince with his shining eyes and carefree laughter. Happiness gave him a look of pride.

Antonio got down from his horse. He stayed for a while with Eusebio, then he left him and rode away along the edge of the marsh.

It was that same evening that Folco decided to try what he had never dared try till now: to mount White Crest and ride him. He chose a moment when he was alone with his horse in the enclosure. He talked to him quietly and stroked him with the flat of his hand all along his flanks.

Folco had no bridle. A rope would have to do. White Crest was shy of this move and resisted at first; then he gave way and allowed Folco to pass the rope around his muzzle.

Standing by the shoulder of his horse, Folco took hold of the mane with both hands, gathered himself and sprang up, landing as lightly as he could on the horse's back.

White Crest reared up in surprise and jumped aside. Folco was speaking to him, but the horse no longer heard his friend's voice; all he knew was that he was a wild horse and his blood was racing because someone had tried to mount him.

In vain Folco gripped with his knees and clutched the mane, with two sudden bucks White Crest got rid of his rider and sent him rolling on the ground.

Folco picked himself up again, bruised and dirty.

White Crest was already a long way away. The boy saw him disappearing at a gallop past the pine-trees.

The beautiful dream was over!

Folco was broken-hearted. If he had not just then seen his grandfather coming to tie up the boat, he would have burst into tears.

And that night, as he lay awake beside his sleeping brother, Folco kept saying under his breath:

'He was my friend. He thought I was going to hurt him. Now he's gone ... and it's my fault. ...'

8 White Crest Disappears

Every day the boy went off in his little boat to comb the marshes, but he was out of luck: he never saw White Crest.

He kept going ashore in the territory of the wild herds. But it was difficult to get within any reasonable distance of the horses.

So two long weeks went by.

One evening, at last, after passing the big lake, and keeping along a bare stretch of bank, Folco caught sight of a band of horses with the light behind them. He moored his boat and jumped out on to the mud. Then, flattening himself behind the clumps of saltwort and crawling through the grass, he began to stalk the horses.

There was no bush to give him cover. Luckily for him, though, the plain was cut by a dry ditch overgrown with grass. The boy slipped down into it and followed its course.

The sun gilded the light coats of the horses, and suddenly they dashed off in a brief gallop, finishing up much closer to Folco. White Crest should have been galloping at the head of his herd but Folco, who would have recognised his friend's proud form at any distance, could not see him there.

Well out of sight in his hiding-place in the ditch, Folco watched the herd for a time. They seemed very restless, huddling close together in a group, as if sensing some sort of danger. They were feeding, pulling up tufts of grass here and there. But they were clearly nervous, ready to fly at the slightest warning.

The horse who acted as sentry was a splendid stallion with a rich black mane and a crest as black as ebony. He stood motionless on tensed legs, his head held high to the wind.

But where was White Crest?

As soon as Folco showed his head above the grass the whole troop of horses fled.

On two more occasions in the days that followed, Folco caught sight of the herd. But White Crest was not among them.

White Crest had quite disappeared. What had become of the fine stallion who was leader of the herd?

If only Folco had been able to confide his anxiety to Antonio! But it was a long time since the old cowboy had called at the cottage.

The wildest ideas came into the boy's mind.

His worst fear was that the cowboys might have captured White Crest; he would have given anything if only he could be sure this was not true.

At last one evening, when he could bear the suspense no longer, instead of going out to the plains as usual, Folco turned his boat towards the high ground beyond the pine-track where the ranch house stood with its stables and corrals.

In the enclosure a young cowboy was training a horse. The unbroken stallion resisted furiously, rearing, trying to tear the reins out of its rider's hands, dashing in all directions. The cowboy's shirt was wet with perspiration, and many times he was nearly unseated. At last he succeeded in mastering the animal and got it running round the enclosure, urging it into a full gallop to release its pent-up feelings. Then he jumped to the ground and came over to the fence.

'Ah, it's you, Folco. Did you want to see Antonio? He's had a bad time in the last few weeks – only just come through it. Come on, young fellow, I'll show you the way.'

Folco followed the cowboy.

He found his old friend lying on a canvas bed. His face looked worn and haggard and his eyes had a feverish glow.

'Hello, lad. I was expecting you to turn up.
You see how it is. My days with horses will soon
be over. . . . Ah, well. Sit down.'

Folco went up to the bed.

'I'm getting well slowly,' said the old man.
'I caught a bad fever. But what about you? Let
me look at you. . . . You don't look very happy.
What is it? Has something happened at home?'

'No,' answered Folco.

Antonio pushed his long, dry fingers through
Folco's mop of hair.

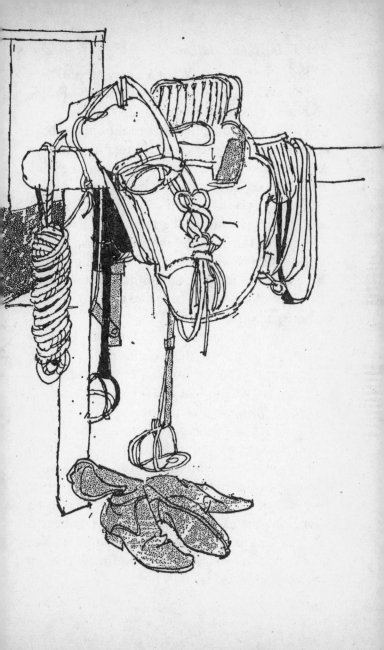

'Speak out, lad. . . . What's worrying you?'

'It's White Crest . . .' stammered Folco. 'White Crest's disappeared.'

The boy confided his fears to the old cowboy, who nodded as he listened. He told him how he had searched the whole marsh and seen the herd several times, but never with its leader.

'I can guess what you must have thought,' said Antonio. 'During the two weeks I've been confined to this bed, the rancher has had two or three young horses caught. But White Crest wasn't one of them. I should have known if he was. The others would have told me.'

'Are you sure, Antonio?'

'Of course I'm sure – if you can ever be absolutely sure of anything in this world.'

'There, you see, Antonio! *If* the rancher has had White Crest caught . . . *If* he's sold him . . .'

'Anything's possible. But frankly I don't think he has. My feeling, you know, is that White Crest has one of his wild moods on him. It all comes from his having suffered so cruelly when he was just a foal. So he provokes the other horses, and fights them. . . . Then off he goes all alone into the plain to chafe and fret by himself. He can't stand the company of the others in this mood, and so he stays away for a time – chasing the wind, they call it.'

Folco listened to the old man.

'That's what I think, lad – I'm telling you for what it's worth. Your White Crest isn't lost, believe me. He's hiding; he'll soon come back to the herd.

But Folco was not convinced. He was still afraid the stallion had suffered some mishap.

'Listen,' said Antonio. 'I've got a proposition to make to you. This'll give you something else to think about. By the end of the week I shall be about again and I'll take you with me to Arles – how's that?'

'To Arles, Antonio?'

'Yes, my boy. Eusebio won't mind – trust me for that. It's carnival time there. You've never left your marshlands before, except for fishing, have you? Well, now you'll see the town, the bull-ring, the bulls, and the fighting. Come then, that's agreed! Sunday I'll call at home for you and take you off with me. Pleased?'

'Oh, yes, Antonio!'

'And don't worry any more, will you? Promise?'

'Promise, Antonio.'

'What a funny boy you are! Off you go – till Sunday. See that you're ready when I come!'

But on the way back home across the marsh it was not of Arles and the carnival that Folco was thinking. No. All his thoughts were with the strange, lone horse, White Crest, the friend of his heart, whom he was afraid he had lost for ever.

9 Carnival at Arles

Sunday came. Faithful to his promise Antonio reined in his horse at Eusebio's cabin in the early dawn.

'We're not going to sprint all the way,' said the old cowboy. 'We'll do it in easy stages. In the first place, there's Franqui to think of.'

'And you'll be stopping to see friends here and there on the way, too,' concluded Grandfather.

'As is right and proper, Eusebio; yes.'

'I shall never get as far as Arles again myself,' sighed the old fisherman. 'Do you remember the last time we went together, Antonio?'

'I should think I do!'

'I remember you in the games and races; you were absolutely fearless.'

'Don't talk about it,' cut in Antonio. 'It's so long ago. Today I'm taking Folco with me. You know your boy will be in good hands. I'm going to show him a bit of the country.'

'Have a good time, Antonio.'

Folco jumped up behind the cowboy on the horse's back. Little brother Rico watched them go, his heart full. Only once before, in the fishing season, had he been separated for a long spell from his older brother. This time he felt that Folco was going off to the other end of the earth.

Just as Antonio had planned, they did the journey in short stages. At night they found food and shelter at the homes of other cowboys, all friends of Antonio. These cowboys were also due to go to Arles, and were busy with their preparations for the big carnival parade. They were polishing their tack; harness leather, bits and curbs glowed with rubbing; stirrups and spurs shone like silver. The visitors were always taken to the stables, for all the men were proud of their horses, and Antonio, as an expert, gave them advice.

The following day they once more took to the road across the tracts of scattered pines. In the distance now and again they caught sight of the dark shapes of bulls with tapering horns. Antonio and Folco rode through vast open stretches of land where the only vegetation was short dry grass here and there.

As Franqui carried them gaily along the track, the two friends chatted all the time.

'I didn't tell Marco we were coming,' said

Antonio. 'I thought I'd give him a surprise.'

Marco lived in a low house in the country near Arles on a stony hillside. Antonio pointed it out to Folco when they were still some way off. Its whitewashed walls stood out clearly amid the silvery verdure of the olive-trees.

Marco, seeing these horsemen climbing the narrow pathway to his house, came out to the stone wall of the terrace to meet them.

'Antonio! What a surprise! And who's the boy? An apprentice you're training for the horses?'

Folco heard only horse-talk all the time he was in the little house with the two old cowboys going back over their memories together.

'It's going to be a fine carnival this year, Antonio,' said Marco. 'We'll have a little siesta and then go down into the town. But you must see to your horse first. Come on, Folco, take Franqui to the stable.'

Franqui gave a happy neigh. And immediately the voice of another horse answered from behind the door.

'It's Rita,' said Marco. 'Yes, that mare I used to have. The gypsies stole her – but of course they had no idea that this little house they passed on their way was where the mare's old master lived! When I saw her, I could hardly believe my eyes. But it was Rita, all right. I shouted her name . . .'

'And she recognised your voice. . . .' said Antonio.

'I wish you could have seen her! She all but broke the shafts and traces! Oh, yes. They'd harnessed her to a cart! Just imagine!'

'So you got her back from them.'

'A crowd gathered in a few seconds,' said Marco. 'Oh, I didn't make a lot of fuss! I mean . . . I'd found Rita again. . . . So I told those scoundrelly horse-thieves . . . I told them they could go and get hanged somewhere else – and quick about it! I didn't have to tell them twice, believe me! Well, come on – a bite for Franqui and then we'll eat, ourselves.'

Folco stroked the neck of White Crest's mother. The boy was delighted that the mare was back with her former master once again.

The carnival was an unforgettable experience for Folco. All the streets were decorated with gay banners and strings of flags flapping in the wind.

'Make way! Make way!'

Black bulls, horns low, dashed through the streets, surrounded by horsemen only just able to control them. They disappeared in a cloud of dust in the direction of the amphitheatre where the bullfights were to take place.

Under a broiling sun, the riders capered on their proud little horses, with their pretty Arlesian girls up behind them wearing embroidered headdresses and decked out like Madonnas. There were all sorts of games, including that very popular one of sticking cockades on the bulls as they rushed past.

Folco, the little fisherboy from the Camargue marshes, was dazzled by the spectacle, the gay crowds, the wild farandole dancing, the musicians nearly bursting their brass instruments – and above all, by the amazing prowess of the horsemen.

'To round off carnival day, Antonio,' said Marco, 'after dinner we'll take your boy to the circus.'

The big top had been set up in the main square of the town. That evening, when the games were over, the circus carts paraded through the streets.

Folco had never been to a circus. Perched high up in the last row of seats, between Antonio and Marco, he watched with wide-open eyes the exciting and fantastic feats that were performed in the brilliantly lighted ring below them.

Clowns, elephants, acrobats, jugglers . . .

And, at last, the horses! A horseman, dressed
with the magnificence of a prince, gave a display
of show-jumping. He rode a huge black horse,
far bigger than any Folco had ever seen in the
Camargue.

Then came the performing cowboys. They
were dressed all in leather, with boots to the top
of their thighs, and wide felt hats; they rushed on
at the gallop after a splendid stallion whose long
white mane swept over his shoulders.

This was a wild horse with no harness on his
snow-white back, and he galloped about the ring

escaping from his pursuers and always avoiding their lassos. But the cowboys closed in and the horse rose up in the midst of them ready to fight them off. He was ready to fight and unseat his enemy as White Crest had done when he jumped at the throat of the rancher's mare.

A cry escaped Folco's lips. He seized Antonio's arm and in a voice trembling with emotion he said:

'Antonio! Do you see?'

'No, it can't be!' exclaimed the old cowboy. He, too, had been struck by the remarkable resemblance.

'Antonio – it is! It's White Crest!'

'No, no, my boy. No . . .'

In the ring, the game went on. The men were still trying to capture the horse. Finally, the lasso caught his two front legs and the superb white stallion was brought down.

'Someone's going to get hurt!' muttered Marco.

But these circus riders knew how to handle horses. They quickly released the stallion from his bonds. He sprang up instantly and, sending the sawdust up in clouds, dashed through the red curtain that covered the entrance to the ring.

'I'm going to make sure and set my mind at rest, all the same,' said Antonio under his breath.

There was a break now before the second half of the performance. People left their seats. Folco and his friends followed the crowd going to visit the animals in the menagerie. There was a tent with a line of cages down each side, and the horses' stalls were right at the end.

'Keep with me,' said Antonio.

Behind the big, ebony-black horse stood the white stallion; he was only just beginning to calm down.

Heart beating fiercely, Folco went up to the stall.

The horse was not White Crest.

The boy felt so relieved, he turned to his old friend and was just about to speak to him when he saw an anxious look come into his eyes. Antonio was staring at three men talking a few yards away from the stall of the white-maned horse.

The one in deerskin boots with a whip in his hand was the ringmaster and manager of the circus. The other two Folco recognised at once; they were the rancher and the young cowboy who had been breaking in a horse that day when Folco had gone to visit Antonio.

'What can they have to talk about, I wonder?' murmured Antonio. 'Are we going to start selling our Camargue horses to the circus now?'

The manager and the rancher were in fierce argument. They waved their arms about, and the rancher appealed to his cowboy to support what he was saying. He pointed to the stall which housed the horse that resembled White Crest.

'This looks bad to me,' muttered Antonio between his teeth.

But Folco paid no attention to his friend's uneasiness. His mind was at rest, for he knew White Crest still roved the marshes of the Camargue. One day, soon, the boy and the stallion would find each other again, and this time they would never be parted.

Folco and Antonio stayed two more days in Marco's little house. Then they had to think of going home.

'When you do decide to leave that rancher of yours,' said Marco, 'you know there's a home waiting for you here.'

'Thank you, Marco,' answered Antonio. 'I won't say no.... But you know what it is, leaving horses....'

'It's hard, Antonio. I know. Well, have a good journey back.'

'Thank you.'

On their return, as when going, Franqui neighed a salute from miles away to the home stables among the trees, long before the riders reached their journey's end. After one last halt at a tiny house near the Rhône, and a whole morning's ride, Folco began to recognise the vast pastures, the old watercourses, almost dry, and the dunes covered with scrub.

Franqui gave a loud whinny when he saw a herd galloping in the distance.

Perhaps it was White Crest's herd! . . .

And so towards evening Antonio and Folco came to the hut with its reed-thatched roof and saw Eusebio and Folco's little brother Rico waving gaily to them.

'This boy will have lots of things to tell you,' Antonio said to them with a laugh. 'And I'm going to stay with you myself tonight – Franqui is worn out. Folco, just put down a bundle of hay in one corner, will you? With that and a blanket I shall be as happy as a king.'

That night they stayed up very late. It was Antonio especially who had a lot to say.

To Folco, now that he had come back to his marsh, all that mattered was that his boat was moored nearby; then tomorrow – and it soon would be tomorrow – he would take up his pole again and be off in search of White Crest, who had perhaps returned to the herd.

10 The Master of the Herds

One evening a few days later the cowboys were all gathered round the rancher's table. They were just finishing dinner. Now Antonio would know soon the meaning of that talk he had over-heard at the circus, between the rancher and the circus manager.

The old man had had this on his mind; he suspected that there was some horse-trading involved. It seemed that the rancher and the circus manager had indeed come to an agreement.

'He wants me to sell him one of our untamed horses,' said the rancher. 'I've got nothing against it, since he's prepared to pay for it.'

Antonio thought to himself that, all things considered, the horses were not really unhappy in the circus – they were well groomed and curry-combed . . .

'Isn't that so, Antonio?'

'Yes, boss, yes. . . .'

'This fellow wants a horse with plenty of spirit. He wants to pep up his lassoing act. He hasn't thought about the damage he'll be in for! He thinks our Camargue horses are no better than mules! He'll soon find out!'

The rancher roared with laughter.

'I've got just the thing,' he said. 'I expect you can guess, eh? You can, anyway, Antonio? No? Well, I'll tell you!'

The rancher took his time. He filled his pipe, lit it, took a long draw, puffed out smoke, then said, still with that nasty smile on his face: 'Yes ... I can assure you this circus fellow's going to get what he wants all right – and better than he bargained for! The horse I have in mind he can hobble as much as he likes before it enters the ring. It won't make any difference! Once it's there it'll let fly! Oho, so he wants a fiery horse, does he!'

This time Antonio and the cowboys guessed their master's intentions.

'What are you all studying your plates for? You want to say something, Antonio? No? Well, listen to me. The horse I intend for this buyer is that foul-tempered stallion who tipped me out of my stirrups – the big white one!'

'Do we have to catch him again?' asked one cowboy, not stopping to think.

'We'll get him,' the rancher replied roughly. 'We've tamed worse.'

Around the table the men were silent.

His voice trembling a little, old Antonio spoke up: 'I think we shall get the better of him, too, if we stick at it long enough,' he said. 'But what about the boy . . . Folco . . .?'

'Hm! Your little savage, you mean?' jeered the rancher. 'What has he got to do with it?'

'It's his horse, boss. You gave it to him.'

'Gave it!' shouted the rancher. 'Good God, man, are you mad? Gave a horse to a boy! I was angry and said any old thing in the heat of the moment, maybe. But even the boy never took it seriously! D'ye hear?'

'You don't know Folco . . .' the old man said. 'White Crest to him . . .'

'Ah! Is that what he calls him: White Crest?' cut in the rancher.

'Yes. White Crest is his horse. When you cursed the stallion and wished it dead, you gave it to the boy.'

'That's enough of this nonsense. Who's the boss here, I'd like to know?'

'But you must listen to me,' said Antonio. 'This is serious, boss. You're a reasonable man—'

'Enough, I say! I've told you. The job starts tomorrow. Everybody ready at daybreak. That's an order. Goodnight!'

The rancher rose from the table and left the

room, slamming the door behind him. His men looked at each other without a word. Antonio went off to the stables with a heavy heart. He had his place in the straw next to Franqui. As the man lay down beside his old companion, the horse stretched his neck and rubbed his nose in the hand that stroked him every night.

'Poor old Franqui, we're all about ready to retire.'

Antonio thought of the grief that awaited his friend Folco. He shared it, too. He felt furious at being old, at not having had the courage to speak out boldly and hold his own with the rancher. Since his trip to Arles, his bad leg had been giving him considerable pain. He had not been on horseback since his return. Close by on a canvas bed lay the young cowboy, sound asleep.

The hours went by.

Lying there on the straw, his eyes fixed on the pale square of the skylight, Antonio tried to contain his feelings of rage and frustration. His mind seethed with anger.

I shall never be able to get into the saddle by myself, he thought.

For he had come to the decision that he would ride over to the fisherman's hut and warn Folco.

'No, I shall never manage it . . . with this leg – it's like a lump of lead,' he told himself as he hobbled up.

He could just manage to saddle Franqui.

'Now, now, don't swell yourself out,' muttered the old man in his horse's ear, as he tightened the girth. Antonio quietly dropped the halter over Franqui's head, then slipped in the bit. The hardest thing was to hoist himself high enough to get into the saddle. 'My arms are useless,' grumbled the old man to himself, '. . . limp as a rag.' He dropped back heavily to the ground.

Franqui, growing impatient, shook himself and in doing so knocked the side of the stall with his hoofs.

'What's that? They're going to fight again!' mumbled the young cowboy, half asleep. He rubbed his eyes, and made to get up and stop the horses fighting.

'Oh, it's you, Antonio. What on earth do you think you're doing going out at this time of night?'

'That's my business . . .'

'That's what you say, Antonio. Come on, now – you're not the boss around here, you know you aren't. The rancher . . .'

'That brute!' cut in Antonio. 'Ah! I'm furious with myself! I should have told him a few home truths last night – I had the chance! Still, they won't lose with keeping!'

'You're worrying yourself all for nothing, Antonio. Keep quiet. That's the best thing you can do!'

'Oh, no!'

'You know you can't beat him. When the boss gets something in his head, have you ever seen him drop it? Well, have you?'

'Listen to me,' said Antonio.

'What do you want to do?'

'Warn the boy.'

'A lot of difference that'll make!'

'Maybe not . . .'

'Well, then?' said the younger man. 'Get back into bed and keep quiet.'

'What's the time!' asked Antonio.

'Not long till dawn now. The moon's very low.'

Antonio was silent. Probably nothing, at this late hour, could help White Crest escape his fate.

But the old man, who, in his anger, was filled with all the fire of his youth, could not stand by idle and do nothing. He felt compelled to warn Folco, and quickly. He was thinking: Franqui hasn't been out for some days. The horse is fresh and would be good for quite a long run. He could go across the marshes with Folco in search of White Crest and with luck, if they found the

wild stallion sooner than the rancher and his men. . .

'Listen,' said Antonio to the young cowboy, 'you can help me into the saddle. You can't refuse me that.'

'If you insist, Antonio.'

'I'm getting heavy. . . . Now then – heave! Thank you.'

'You've barely got time, Antonio.'

'I know,' said the old man.

When he got past the gates of the stables, Antonio urged Franqui to a gallop.

Over in the east the sky was lightening. Along the horizon ran a pale, thin line, blurred in a fine mist. The birds were beginning to wake up. A flight of ducks skimmed over the bushes. For as long as the ground was solid beneath his horse's feet, Antonio let him gallop freely. At the first ponds and stretches of marsh they had to slow down.

Already the sun was rising, throwing into relief the black silhouettes of the pines.

Antonio, after crossing the wide plain where the white flowers grew, came in sight of Folco's hut. A thin line of smoke went up from it into the branches of the trees.

The boy was up already. He must be making coffee by the fire.

No time to lose. . . .

His horse, under his urging, thrust on knee-deep in mud, until at last they came to the door of the tiny house. Antonio shouted:

'Folco! Folco!'

There was no answer. Then after a few moments:

'Coming, Antonio, coming!'

It was the voice of the old fisherman.

'Isn't Folco there?' asked Antonio.

'Didn't you see him?' said the grandfather. 'He left only a minute ago.'

'In his boat?'

'Yes, in his boat, of course. We are fishing folk, you know, Antonio,' added the old man with a laugh.

But Antonio had no wish to laugh at that moment. His last hope was fast disappearing. Which way must he go to find Folco in the marshes now?

'Was there something you wanted to tell the boy, then?' asked the grandfather.

'No, nothing,' answered Antonio. 'See you some day soon. . . .'

And setting Franqui at a trot, he plunged off into the marsh again without any idea which direction to take.

11 Like a Beautiful Dream

White Crest that morning was returning in search of his herd. Where he had been in his lonely wanderings no one would ever know.

If Folco had pushed his boat towards the river he would have seen the proud stallion's form outlined at the top of the dunes. White Crest, his mane in the wind, looked down from there upon the dull wastes that stretched away and away, dotted with strings of pools; this was his domain. Instinct told him where to look for the herd which he had come back to lead again. His whinny startled a flock of tiny birds. They rose up and spread like a handful of millet scattered in the air. Then the horse ran down the slope of the dunes towards the marsh.

This time luck was on Folco's side. He had no idea that the longed-for meeting was so near. Nor did White Crest realise, as he cut across the plain, that he was running towards his friend.

But he was also going towards the rancher's men. In the saddle since dawn, the horsemen, directed by their master, had set out to patrol the whole stretch of the marsh. One went ahead as scout to find the herd and came back with the news that White Crest was not with the other horses. Spaced out in a line, like beaters at a hunt, the cowboys advanced across the marsh, searching any bushes and high reeds where a horse might have hidden.

The first rider to sight the stallion alerted the rest.

'There he is! Ahead of us. Right in the sun!'

The men had just time to glimpse a white flash like a streak of white cloud vanishing across the watery plain.

'He's ours!' cried the rancher.

The man expected the horse to try to escape by running away. If White Crest did that he was bound to lose, for the horsemen would keep up with him until he was exhausted. It was always easy for the riders to cut off the retreat of an excited, frightened horse.

But, as if he guessed their game, instead of dashing off at full gallop for the plain, White Crest made straight for the cover of a patch of marsh where the reeds grew thick. He was sure of finding a place to hide in that dense tangle of long stems and spear-shaped leaves which grew higher than a man on horseback. White Crest plunged right into the heart of the reeds.

Folco sat in his boat only a hundred yards away but he had not even seen the horsemen. He was winding between the mudbanks where thick clumps of reeds blocked his view.

'This way!' shouted the boss.

And he gave his orders.

'We'll have to smoke the animal out! Fire's the only way of getting him out of there. . . . Jump to it, boys! Set fire to each corner of this patch!'

The men sprang to the ground and used their lighters. Soon long flames began licking over the reeds and flared up quickly.

'Stand away, boys! We only have to wait for him to come out now!' the rancher cried.

The horsemen climbed back into the saddle, ready to give chase.

Alerted by the shouts, Folco saw the smoke rising from the marsh. Then he caught sight of the men on horseback and their boss shouting his orders. Instantly he understood what was happening. The men were out to capture a horse – and Folco could see that horse some way away, leaping about behind the flames and dropping back into the reeds neighing with terror.

It was White Crest! White Crest had sought

shelter in the reeds and the tangle of bushes where the men could not follow.

But men were always the stronger in the end. The rancher meant to show him that. Now the cowboys waited for the stallion to show himself. They were sure of seeing him as soon as he came out of the ring of flames, blinded by the smoke. But White Crest, instead of taking flight, thrust deeper and deeper into the marsh.

Folco jumped from his boat and ran breathlessly towards the fire, splashing up mud in all directions. He slipped and fell, then scrambled up again, plastered with mud.

The riders had not seen him yet. Now, as they watched the fire they had unleashed sweeping wildly away, they were frightened; they were no longer its masters. The men had not taken the strength of the wind into account. They had not foreseen the vast, raging blaze, that was rushing right across the march. It darted over the ground, licking at the reeds and instantly setting them alight like long red torches whose flames the wind drove flat.

The men were not going to ride their horses through this bonfire! And the stallion was a prisoner inside the ring, in serious danger of perishing in the flames! Of course, that had not been the rancher's intention. But it looked as if

nothing could save the proudest stallion of his
herd.

Like the horsemen, Folco had immediately
realised the danger for his friend White Crest.
On he ran across the watery plain, with only one
thought in his mind – to save White Crest.

Folco reached the barrier of flames, but how
could he find a way through them? The boy lay
down in the water and crept forward on his
stomach between the clumps of burnt reeds,
feeling his way along a narrow ditch of mud.
His hair scorched, his hands burnt, he succeeded
in passing through the hedge of fire. Then he
ran through the reeds, shouting desperately:

'White Crest!'

A long cry answered him.

The boy could not see three yards in front of
him in the suffocating smoke, and the fire was
spreading. In the red darkness Folco with
difficulty made his way towards the spot where
he had heard the stallion neighing, and at last he
saw White Crest, surrounded by flames. The
terrified horse trampled about wildly in his own
tracks, breaking down the reeds. Maddened,
choked, and blinded by the smoke, the animal
was in a state of panic.

Folco approached him. The proud creature
may have felt that salvation could come only

from his friend who had thrown himself into the fire and through the blazing marsh in order to save him. The stallion trembled in every limb, yet he allowed Folco to stroke him and seize his mane.

In one leap Folco was on his back. Instinctively the horse shied. But he did not try to throw his young rider.

'Come on! Come on!'

Folco spurred White Crest on with his bare heels.

'Come on, White Crest! Come on!'

Both Folco and the horse were choking in the smoke. The horse took a great leap to clear a blazing patch. Flames enclosed the entire marsh. Twice White Crest shied at the wall of fire – and twice Folco talked quietly into his ear and stroked him before bringing him back again to face the flaming barrier.

At last, urged on, and trying to obey this determined boy who seemed to be afraid of nothing himself, White Crest jumped the wall, the hairs of his crest and mane being scarcely scorched at all.

The rancher and his men were stupefied when they saw this boy, black with smoke, come flying over the bank of flames, crouching low on the neck of his horse and rushing away at breakneck speed.

'You see, he got him! The horse you gave him!' shouted Antonio, who had just come up to join the group of watchers. 'He even went into the fire to find him!'

Poor old Antonio! Did he really think that because the little fisherboy had shown so much courage the rancher would make good his promise? That would have been to misjudge the man's nature.

'Quick! Cut them off!' shouted the rancher. 'They won't get far.'

It was the first time Folco had had his beautiful horse between his legs. White Crest ran like the wind. But when they came to the slopes of the dunes, the stallion had to slacken his pace, for his feet sank deep into the loose sand.

The pursuing riders were gaining on them. Folco could clearly hear their voices.

'Faster, White Crest! Faster!'

The horse put out all his strength. But his inexperienced rider hampered his progress. Though Folco clung to the mane with all his might, he could not help rolling from side to side on the horse's back. Several times he only just missed falling right off.

It was a wild ride. In the hollows between the dunes White Crest kept gaining. Instinctively he veered towards the marsh, but the cowboys always blocked his way. Folco heard the rough breathing of his mount as the strength of the stallion began to flag.

'We've got him!' shouted the rancher.

White Crest came headlong down the slope. Carried down in a sand-slide, he dug in all four feet to brake the descent. At the bottom he discovered a narrow strip of solid ground and dashed forward again at a gallop.

Folco, his bare legs clamped against the flanks of his horse, holding his breath, intoxicated with the speed, gave himself up completely to the excitement of this wonderful ride. The young fisherboy had almost forgotten that enemies were after him, hounding him down.

White Crest sped away of his own accord as soon as a horseman drew near. His wild-horse instinct guided him in evading his pursuers.

'Keep going, White Crest!'

At the end of the narrow strip of land the marsh widened. That way lay their only hope.

Tearing on at top speed, White Crest just managed to swerve clear of one of his pursuers as the man came out suddenly from behind the dunes. Ahead the way was free.

All at once, just as White Crest was gathering himself for a jump across a wide ditch, another horseman appeared right in his path as he was about to jump.

It was Antonio on Franqui. The old cowboy swerved his horse aside to leave the way open.

'Folco!'

Antonio would have let the boy pass. He only wanted Folco to know a friend was near. But Folco never heard the voice of his friend, for it was drowned by a long neigh from White Crest. The boy barely saved himself from flying off his horse and sprawling on the ground as White Crest faltered under him and stopped dead at the ditch. Then, turning back sharply, the stallion set off again at a gallop.

This time the struggle was no longer even. Soon White Crest would have no breath left, and in the sand along the foot of the dunes he found the going hard.

The cowboys rallied to the rancher's call and followed his orders; gradually they surrounded the stallion, with the boy clutching his mane. The boss came out into one of the dips between the sandhills. Digging his spurs into his mare, he urged her on, though she was half blinded by the dust thrown up by White Crest's hoofs.

His men followed him.

Far to the rear Antonio rode as hard as he could to try to catch up. He was filled with foreboding when he saw the boss and his men already rejoicing, confident of victory.

There was no way for the wild horse to escape; instinctively he had sought to flee into the marshes. Now the horse and his child rider turned straight towards the Rhône. They would have to stop when they came to the river; it was too wide to cross. There they would be caught.

Folco could hear the shouts of the men as they urged on their horses. He suddenly saw ahead of him the great sheet of shimmering water. Waves rippled like prairie-grass in the wind.

White Crest did not slacken his pace. Through all this wild race Folco had let his horse lead him. He did nothing to hold him back. White Crest galloped on right to the water's edge.

The shouts came nearer, shouts of men, whom the horse hated, who always had hunted him and been his enemies. The horse plunged into the river and at once began to swim, with the boy on his back still clinging to his mane.

The swift current bore them forward, the beautiful white stallion and his inseparable friend, the fisherboy who loved horses. They were far out in the river when the men came to the bank and halted behind the boss. They all saw the danger Folco was in.

Frightened and struck with remorse, the rancher shouted with all his might:

'Come back, lad, come back! You can have the horse. He's yours!'

'Folco! Folco!' all the men shouted.

It was too late.

The fisherboy loved this wonderful white horse more than anything in the world, and he knew that these men had once lied to him. Probably Folco did not even hear the desperate cries of the horsemen, now powerless to rescue him. Tossed on the swell, his hair plastered over his eyes and one arm around White Crest's neck, Folco let himself be carried along on the current that swept to the sea.

'Folco! Folco! Come back!'

The last voice which he might have heard was that of his old friend, Antonio.

But the boy was far away now, lost in the lapping of the waves. He listened only to the dull roar of the water, like the sound that echoes in a big shell held to the ear.

From the bank the men soon could distinguish no more than a white speck: the head of the horse, White Crest, as he still swam with the boy's cheek pressed against his own. Then even the white speck faded from sight and the watching men could see nothing but the waves.

Folco, still clinging to his horse's neck, felt numbness steal upon him, deep drowsiness.

The water streamed over his face.

He closed his eyes. On he floated, as in a dream, clinging to his friend White Crest, from whom he would never be parted.

They swam on for a long, long time. . . .

The singing waters of the Rhône, rocking them gently, carried them both away on the current of the great river to the shores of a land where children and horses are for ever friends.

More Beaver Books

We hope you have enjoyed this Beaver Book. Here are some of the other titles:

About Jumping A Beaver original. The fourth in the Young Riders Guides series by Robert Owen and John Bullock. Illustrated with black and white photographs and line drawings

Dark Fury An exciting story about the last great wild stallion of the American West by Joseph E. Chipperfield, author of *Ghost Horse*, also in Beavers

Desperate Journey Martluk the Eskimo boy finds that rescue is dependent on him when the plane in which he is travelling with three middle-aged Americans crashes in the frozen forests of Arctic Canada. A gripping novel by the explorer J. M. Scott

Everybody's Birthday Book A Beaver original. A day-by-day account by George and Cornelia Kay of the famous people and important events that share your birthday, complete with charts on which to record friends' birthdays

New Beavers are published every month and if you would like the *Beaver Bulletin* – which gives all the details – please send a large stamped addressed envelope to:

Beaver Bulletin
The Hamlyn Group
Astronaut House
Feltham
Middlesex TW14 9AR

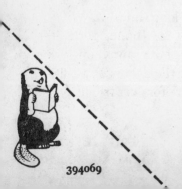